Scholastic Publications Ltd.,
10 Earlham Street, London WC2H 9RX, UK

Scholastic Inc.,
730 Broadway, New York, NY 10003, USA

Scholastic Tab Publications Ltd.,
123 Newkirk Road, Richmond Hill,
Ontario L4C 3G5, Canada

Ashton Scholastic Pty. Ltd.,
P O Box 579, Gosford, New South Wales,
Australia

Ashton Scholastic Ltd.,
165 Marua Road, Panmure, Auckland 6,
New Zealand

First published by Scholastic Publications Limited, 1988
Text copyright © John Cunliffe, 1988
Illustrations copyright © Scholastic Publications Limited and
Woodland Animations Limited, 1988
Reprinted 1989

ISBN 0 590 70908 9

Made and printed in Belgium
Typeset in Times Roman by AKM Associates (UK) Ltd.,
Ajmal House, Hayes Road, Southall, London

Postman Pat's
Cat-up-a-Tree
Party

Story by **John Cunliffe** Pictures by **Joan Hickson**
From the original Television designs by **Ivor Wood**

Hippo Books
in association with André Deutsch

It was a sunny day in spring. Pat was
sitting in the garden having a cup of tea.
Julian was playing on his bike. Sara had
her bike out; she was mending a
puncture. Jess was . . . where *was* Jess?

He wasn't in the house. He wasn't on the grass. He wasn't on the wall, where he liked to lie in the sun. Then, they all heard,

"Miaow! Miaow!"

That must be Jess. But where was he? Pat looked everywhere, but he couldn't see Jess.

"Miaow! Miaow!"

"Jess! Jess!" Pat called. "Can anybody see Jess? I can hear him, but I can't see him."

"*Miaow! Miaow!*" went Jess, and they all looked for him.

"He's up there," said Julian.

"Where?" said Pat.

"In the sky," said Julian.

"He must be flying after the birds," said Sara.

"Now I know Jess can do a lot of things, but I'm sure he cannot fly," said Pat. "And he sounds upset about something. I think we'd better find him."

"Look," said Sara. "There he is!" Sara pointed. High up in the pine tree at the bottom of the garden, a furry face looked down at them. They could just see Jess clinging to a branch and lashing his tail, and miaowing sadly.

"Nay, Jess, what are you doing up there?" said Pat. "Are you playing at being a squirrel? Come on down, and you can have a saucer of cream."

But Jess stayed where he was, and miaowed . . . so sadly.

"Poor Jess," said Julian. "What's to do with you?"

"I don't think he *can* get down," said
Sara. "I think he's stuck. Don't you
remember, he was stuck up a tree once
before. It was when Alf's pig got into our
garden, and we chased it all over the
place. Jess went up the apple tree that
time, and you had to get the ladder to get
him down. But this tree's a lot higher."

"Bless us, I never thought he'd do it
again, though," said Pat. "And, oh
dear . . . I've just remembered. I lent the
ladder to Ted so he could paint his house.
Now what are we going to do?"

"Can't you climb up and bring him
down?" said Julian.

10

Pat tried to climb the pine tree, but the branches were so close together that he couldn't even begin. And all the time Jess was miaowing that he wanted to come down.

Sara brought a chair out, and Pat stood on it and reached up for Jess; but Jess was too far away. Sara brought a table out. Pat put the chair on the table, and held everything steady, and Sara climbed up, first on to the table, then on to the chair, to reach for Jess.

She might just have been able to reach him, but the table began to wobble, and Sara grabbed at the tree, and made the tree shake. Jess took fright, and went even farther up the tree. Now no one could reach him. Sara jumped down, and now she felt so wobbly that she had to sit down with a cup of tea till she felt better.

"We shouldn't climb up on chairs and tables," she said. "We could have a nasty accident."

"Well," said Pat, "it was you that brought the table and chair out."

"Hm," said Sara. "I'll not do that again in a hurry. It gave me a real fright. I know just how Jess feels, up in the top of that tree."

"I don't know why he doesn't just turn round and come down backwards," said Pat.

"It's odd," said Sara. "Cats are marvellous at going up trees, but hopeless at coming down again. It just seems that they can't do it. It's a wonder that all the trees aren't full of cats."

14

Just then, Doctor Gilbertson came by in her red Sierra. She stopped to see what they were all doing, standing staring up into a tree. She thought perhaps they had found a rare bird, and brought her camera, hoping to get a picture. She took a picture anyway.

"It'll do for the Animals Section in the Camera Club competition," she said.

"Never mind your competition, doctor," said Pat. "What are we going to do about getting Jess down? He can't stay up there for ever."

"Oh, it just needs a little thought, Pat," said the doctor. "There's not much we doctors can't cure. I'll soon prescribe a remedy. Now, let's see. I'll need a box, a long stick, some string, nails, and some cat food."

"This tea's cold," said Pat. "I'll brew a fresh pot while you're busy. Now I think I can lay my hands on a good long stick, and we have plenty of boxes, and string . . . won't be a jiffy, doctor."

They soon had fresh tea on the table. Doctor Gilbertson fixed the box to the end of the stick, and put some of Jess's favourite food in it.

"There you are," she said, "that should do it. The patient should be down and about in no time at all.

"You see, all we have to do is to hold the box up on the end of the stick. Jess will smell the food, jump into the box, and we will lower him safely to the ground."

Doctor Gilbertson poked the box up into the tree. Jess looked at it suspiciously, miaowed, but did not move.

"My arms are too short," said the doctor. "I'm not holding it high enough. You try, Pat, you'll do better."

Pat pushed the box higher into the tree, and they all talked to Jess.

"Come on, Jess. Come on, puss. Get in the box, Jess. You'll be all right. Come on, then, Jess."

But it was no good. Jess did not move.

"Have a fresh cup of tea," said Pat, "while we have another think. I don't think Jess will get in that box."

The Reverend Timms called with the parish magazine. "Are you having a garden party?" said the Reverend.

"Sort of," said Sara. "Come and have a cup of tea."

"Thank you. Lovely. Hello, what's Jess doing up there?" said the Reverend.

"Just sitting there," said Sara. "You could call it a cat-up-a-tree party as well. A new kind. You see, Reverend, Jess is stuck up the tree, and we're all trying to get him down. Doctor kindly stopped to help, but her idea isn't working. Jess just won't get in the box."

"Well, no, I don't think I'd get in a box on the end of a stick if I were Jess," said the Reverend. "Would you?"

"Well, not being a cat, I don't know," said the doctor. "Have you any good ideas, Reverend?"

"I'm afraid the Bible says little about cats, and nothing, as far as I know, about cats in trees. What we need is your ladder."

"Ted's borrowed it," they all answered.

"Can't we go and borrow it back?" said the Reverend. "It would fit in the doctor's Sierra, with the back open."

"Ted's gone to see his sister in Carlisle, and won't be back 'til late," said Pat. "He's sure to have locked the ladder up safely in his shed."

"Oh dear, what a bother," said the Reverend. "There must be someone else with a ladder in Greendale."

"Alf has one," said Pat, "but it's sure to be too short."

Now there was the sound of a tractor in the road.

It was Peter Fogg. He saw the crowd of people talking and drinking tea, so he stopped to join in. They told him about Jess, and he had a good look.

"Come down, you silly cat," he said to Jess, but it did no good. "I know," he said, "I'll get him down with my tractor."

"Have a cup of tea while you're thinking about it," said Sara. "How can you get a cat out of a tree with a tractor?"

"Thanks," said Peter. "Just what I need. It should be easy to get Jess down. I have the digger on the tractor, and it goes really high on the hydraulic gear. I'll put it as high as it can go, then drive up to your hedge with the bucket as near to that tree as I can get it. Then Jess can jump into the bucket, and I can lower it gently to the ground."

"He wouldn't jump into a box on the end of a stick," said Doctor Gilbertson. "And how's that cough of yours?"

"Oh, a lot better, thanks, doctor," said Peter. "But a tractor's bucket's different from a box. It's a lot bigger, for one thing."

"It's worth a try, I suppose," said the doctor. "Now don't you forget to come for some more medicine if that cough starts up again. All right, stand back everybody. We're going to try again."

There was a roar as the tractor started up, and they all saw the large bucket coming over the hedge.

Jess had such a fright when he saw it that he went still farther up the tree! And then Pat saw what was going to happen, and he shouted, "Stop, Peter, stop!"

But the engine was making such a noise that Peter didn't hear him. There was a great crunching and grinding sound, and the tractor came right through the hedge. Oh dear, what a mess there was!

"What happened?" shouted Sara.

"Ooh, I am sorry," said Peter. "I was so busy watching Jess and the tree that I forgot there was a hedge in the way. I've made quite a big hole in it, haven't I?"

Just then, Mrs Pottage and the twins came along. Sara gave them a cup of tea each and told them what had happened.

"Don't worry about the hedge," said Mrs Pottage. "We have plenty of spare fence posts in our barn. Peter can bring some round tomorrow and mend that hole."

The cat-up-a-tree party was getting bigger and bigger. Mrs Goggins came next, then Alf and Dorothy Thompson. Pat dashed indoors to get the best tea service out, and Sara brewed more tea.

Julian filled the sugar-basin, and Katy and Tom helped him to hand biscuits round.

George Lancaster came with two dozen eggs, and Miss Hubbard, passing on the way to the church to arrange the flowers, stopped to see what was going on. Not one of them could think of a way of getting Jess down from the tree.

"We'll soon have all Greendale in our garden," said Sara. "It's a good thing this doesn't happen every day. We'd never have enough biscuits to go round."

Then Ted arrived back from Carlisle, and called to ask Pat if he would like to go fishing in his boat next Saturday. They were telling him to go for the ladder, all at the same time, and he was trying to work out why they wanted a ladder at that time of day, and someone dropped a cup just as the kettle started to whistle yet again, and there was a fine old rumption, when Granny Dryden walked up the garden path. She banged her stick on the path, and stopped them all in their tracks.

"Whatever is going on?" she demanded to know.

"Well, it's Jess, you see . . ." Pat began.

"Do sit down and have a cup of tea and a cake," said Sara.

"Thank you very much," said Granny Dryden. "Is it a party? Is it Jess's birthday party?"

"Well, no, not really," said Pat. "I know it looks like a party, but . . ."

"Where is Jess? I haven't seen him today at all."

"That's what we're trying to tell you," said Sara. "Jess is up that tree and he's stuck, and we've all been trying to get him down."

"Trying to get him down? Keeping him up more like! Poor Jess, up that tree all this time." Granny Dryden sounded cross.

"We've tried our best to get him down," said Pat. "Honestly, Granny Dryden, we have done our best. Ted's going to get the ladder, and we'll soon have Jess down now."

"That cat's too high for any ladder," said Granny Dryden. "But if you all do as I say, he'll soon be down. And you won't need any ladder."

"Can you get him down, Granny Dryden?" said Mrs Goggins, astonished.

"Of course I can," said Granny Dryden rather sharply. "I've seen cats in trees before any of you were born. It's an old tale, that one about cats not being able to get down from trees; and it's not true. It's just folks making a fuss and a stir that gets them into a state, and they just won't come down, then. Jess will never come down with all this coming and going. If you all go home and get your tea, Jess will come down in his own good time. You'll see."

"It's the wisdom of age," said the Reverend Timms. "I think we should all try taking Granny Dryden's advice. Our Lord works in mysterious ways."

"It's just commonsense," said Granny Dryden, "that's all. Away you go home, every last one of you, and you'll see that I'm right."

One by one, they all went home.

"But will *you* stay, and come in for some tea, Granny Dryden?" said Sara.

"Only if you let me help with the washing up," said Granny Dryden. "You must have a right bonny pile of it."

They had, and it took a good long time to get it all washed, and dried, and put away. But they had a good tea, with toast, and crumpets, and scones. And they had a good talk about all the news of the valley.

All this time, Jess had the garden, and the tree, to himself. Apart from the birds, that is, and they didn't like it a bit, having a cat in their tree. But it was much quieter now that everyone had gone, and Jess was beginning to feel really hungry. He thought he might just try his claws to see if they would hold him going backwards. He got down one branch. There was more tumbling in it than climbing, and this was a very scratchy tree. Down another branch. Ouch! It was also a prickly tree. Another branch. Slowly, very slowly, Jess was working his way down the tree.

In the house, Sara was saying, "I hope
our Jess is all right. Do you think I
should pop out and see how he's getting
on?"

But Granny Dryden said, "Certainly not! He will get on much better without anyone fussing round him. You'll see. Just get on with your tea, and you'll soon see your Jess safe and sound. He's a clever cat. He can take care of himself. We had a cat like Jess when I was a young lass. It could have been his great-grandad. He was always going up trees. I remember once. . ." And Granny Dryden told them a story of long ago.

All this time, Julian was hiding behind
the curtains, peeping out into the garden.
He couldn't see Jess, because the pine
tree's needles and branches hid him. But
he could see the tree shaking as Jess
tumbled his way down it. And he could
see the startled birds fussing and scolding
at Jess. The shaking crept closer and
closer to the ground. At last, a very
rumpled cat jumped from the lowest
branch on to the grass, and ran to the
house, to scratch at the door to be let in.
And, oh! what a fuss they all made of
him!

"There you are!" said Granny Dryden. "I told you he'd do it! Good old Jess. Just like his great-grandad. *Clever* Jess."

Jess jumped on her knee, and she cuddled him and stroked him, and he soon began to purr. Pat, and Sara, and Julian gave him a cuddle, and then Jess asked politely for his tea. Sara opened a tin of sardines for him as a special treat.

"Look at his fur," said Pat. "He looks as though he's been through a hedge backwards!"

"He's done better," said Julian. "He's been through a tree backwards."

The tree had rubbed Jess's fur the wrong way; it was sticking out in all directions, and it was full of pine-needles that itched and prickled.

"I know what he is," said Granny Dryden. "One of these people they talk about on the television. What do they call them . . . *punks*, is that it? Yes, he's Jess the Punk Cat."

"Oh, poor old Jess!" said Sara. "He looks like an unmade bed. He needs a good brushing. That'll get the needles out, and then he'll feel a lot better. Won't you, Jess?"

Jess didn't like being brushed, but it did get the needles out, and he did feel better. Well enough, indeed, to go looking for mice after tea, in Mrs. Pottage's barn. But it was a long time, a very long time, before he climbed a tree again.